E
c632m

Mr. Jordan in the Park

Mr. Jordan in the Park

Laura Jane Coats

Macmillan Publishing Company   New York
Collier Macmillan Publishers   London

Macmillan Publishing Company
866 Third Avenue, New York, NY 10022
Collier Macmillan Canada, Inc.
Printed and bound in Japan
First American Edition

10 9 8 7 6 5 4 3 2 1

The text of this book is set in 18 point Simoncini Garamond.
The illustrations are rendered in watercolor.

Library of Congress Cataloging-in-Publication Data
Coats, Laura Jane. Mr. Jordan in the park/
Laura Jane Coats.—1st American ed.
p.   cm.
Summary: Reviews the entire life of Mr. Jordan,
especially happy times in his favorite place, the park,
where he now still enjoys quieter good times in his old age.
ISBN 0-02-719053-6
[1. Old age—Fiction. 2. Parks—Fiction.] I. Title.
PZ7.C6293Mr 1989   [E]—dc19   88-13295 CIP   AC

for
Thomas
Jordan

Mr. Jordan loves
to go to the park.
All his life it has been
his favorite place.

When he was a baby,
he rode there in a carriage.
He liked to feel
the warm sun on his face.

After he had learned to walk,
he fed bread crumbs
to the birds in the park.

Later he sailed his boat at the fountain.

Then he shot marbles

and raced his bicycle through the park.

He flew his kite on the open lawn.

When he was older,
he played baseball in the park.

As a young man,
he went rowing on the lake

and walked through the park
in the moonlight.

In time he was married
and took his family
on picnics in the park.

He pushed his son on the swing
at the playground

and waved as he whirled by
on the carousel.

Now Mr. Jordan is old.

He listens to concerts in the park
on Sunday afternoons.

He goes bowling on the green

or meets a friend for a game of chess.

Some days he sits quietly
on a park bench.
He likes to feel
the warm sun on his face

and watch the life around him.